A ROOKIE READER

EAT YOUR PEAS, LOUISE!

By Pegeen Snow

Illustrations by Mike Venezia

Prepared under the direction of Robert Hillerich, Ph.D.

SCHOLASTIC INC.

New York   Toronto   London   Auckland   Sydney
Mexico City   New Delhi   Hong Kong   Buenos Aires

To MARION RICHARDSON
aunt, friend, poet

ISBN 0-516-23796-9

25 24 23 22   11/0

Printed in China.   62

First Scholastic printing, October 2001

"Eat your peas, Louise.
You will like good peas like these." 3

"How fat and round they are!
Just squeeze!"

5

"Will you eat them if
I add some cheese?"

"Eat them with your fork, or. . ."

"Eat them with your spoon."

"But eat them up fast.
It's way past noon."

"Eat them and you may fish with me."

16

"Or climb a tree."

"Or watch TV."

19

"Eat them when I count to three."

"One. . . two. . ."

"Oh, me!"

"Don't be a tease, Louise!
Eat your peas!"

"Please?"